Dulcinea: The Calico Queen

Written by
J Camila Vogel

Illustrated by
Cathy McDearmid

This book is dedicated to Barton Joseph with gratitude beyond
the moon for his love and dedication to creative pursuits.

CHAPTER 1: HAWKS' HAVEN

*M*y attendants were tossing and turning all night long! As soon as I managed to find a comfortable position to lie in, I would suddenly find myself thrown to a different part of the bed, and once, even onto the floor! Can you imagine?

It felt like an eternity before I finally managed to rouse my attendant from her deep slumber. After the terrible night of torment I had suffered, I wanted to be free to roam my kingdom before first light. She groaned as I prowled on top of her, pawing at the blankets, trying to wake her up. She even tried to swat me away in an attempt to sleep longer. That only made me meow louder. At this point, I did not care if I was disturbing her; after all, it was she who had kept me awake all night with her restless sleep, and now I wanted out!

Although she is the best attendant I have ever had, and perhaps the finest in all the lands from one sea to the next, that is not an excuse for the way she disrupted my beauty sleep. I do not enjoy having my sleep disturbed with worry over *her* well-being.

Finally, she picked me up in her loving arms and whispered softly in my ears, "My precious Dulcinea, I am so sorry for making you wait for your morning walk." She snuggled my face as I looked at her warily. This was her peace offering. I am not usually quick to forgive but how could I ignore her? I licked her hand in return. No matter how much she annoyed me, I found it hard to resist her love and found myself returning it no matter what. She gave me a quick squeeze and then gently placed me outside the back door.

My attendant came into my life about six years ago, on a dark Christmas night. I was really impressed because she instantly liked me and cared about my happiness. I let her hold and pet me right away, and I've never regretted that decision. She has always been very loyal to me, right from the beginning.

In fact, ever since she joined me, my kingdom, Hawks' Haven, has grown much bigger and expanded far more than I could have imagined. There are now vast orchards filled with delicious fruits, winding pathways to explore, and tall walls surrounding it all. These walls are there to keep out those noisy and smelly dogs who tend to leave their personal droppings for everyone to see and smell. Dogs can be quite crude, always rushing around without thinking about anyone else, with no care in the world for whom they might hurt or bother.

During my morning walk, I strolled along the winding pathways which were lined with vibrant and lush green plants. These plants were covered in fresh morning dew, which gathered on their leaves in tiny, sparkling pools, reflecting against the sun brightly like jewels. As I went along, I lapped up this dew and discovered that each leaf had a different and unique scent and taste, making it a delightful morning treat.

In the midst of my peaceful morning thoughts, suddenly, a long black cat named Capo landed squarely onto my back with a thud. "For heaven's sake, can't anyone have a few quiet moments in the morning without having to entertain you?" I hissed, both startled and angered by the sudden assault. I quickly pushed Capo off me and gave his backside a swat as he scampered away.

He landed with a thud, blinking his big eyes like nothing had happened.

"Sorry about that, Your Majesty, I thought you were a tortoise from behind . . . you know, something slow to play with . . . How are things looking and tasting in the kingdom this morning?"

I felt the fur on my back stand tall.

"How RUDE! A TORTOISE! You can't even keep your four white paws clean."

Certainly, I thought that I must show this young, foolish cat a better way than scolding him. After all, I've been told that when viewed from the backside, I do resemble a tortoiseshell cat. But in truth, I'm a calico cat with a magnificent blend of colors and the softest fur you can imagine. I take great pride in keeping my fur immaculately clean and tidy.

The pristine whiteness of my fur stands out beautifully against the backdrop of my coat, which features striking shades of black, brown, and vibrant orange, creating a tortoiseshell-like appearance. Specifically, my nose, front bib, full belly, and all four of my paws boast this exquisite white fur, making for a striking and memorable contrast.

"It's not his fault; he simply does not know what true beauty is." I thought to myself.

Life in Hawks' Haven had been peaceful and content until the arrival of the great hunter Capo, who proudly displayed his hunting skills and showed off his prowess at every turn, jumping on every opportunity to be the center of attention.

His acrobatic feats, like flipping a squirrel midair while perched on a narrow, ten-foot-high wall, caught all our attention.

Mr. Capo's generous offerings of various rodents and birds stirred up a mix of excitement and concern among us. It became the talk of the Haven, as everyone was captivated and marveled by his hunting skills.

The sight of him effortlessly snatching birds from the sky with his extraordinarily long and strong arms left us both amazed and astonished. We could hardly stop discussing his striking abilities.

However, there was a downside to all this fascination. Capo's playful antics and hunting displays had everyone so engrossed that they began to forget their responsibilities, especially their duty to take care of me. It was a shocking realization, and I watched in horror as they got carried away, seemingly forgetting their essential tasks. The Haven, once a place of harmony, had become a theater of distraction, with my people forgetting their ultimate responsibility: ME!

In a short span of time, Capo's playful antics had secured him a permanent role in Hawks' Haven as both a skilled hunter and an entertainer. His impressive performances earned him a stylish and brilliantly colorful collar that proudly declared his important role and high station in Hawks' Haven.

As for me, I've had to learn to avert my gaze so that the people here can fully enjoy the joyful entertainment he provides. The truth is, I can hardly stand to look at him, despite his exceptional handsomeness. He's just about grown into his sleek and solid body, which is adorned with a luxuriously smooth short black fur coat. His long white whiskers against his mostly black body create a striking and captivating sight. There are also a few tasteful small patches of white on each of his four paws, a little on his chin, and a remarkable diamond-shaped patch on his chest.

To be honest, in some of my past lives, I might have found it hard to resist the charms of this muscular show-off. However, these days, I cannot stand the sight of him because all of his hunting skills have caused a great loss of life, peace, and joy, as the birds are now all too afraid to come to Hawks' Haven.

CHAPTER 2: DULCINEA'S PREVIOUS LIVES

In my very first life, my royal status became obvious when I was given a small kingdom at a young age. I had a kind but elderly attendant who had no children of his own. When he passed away, I was sent off on a unique quest of my own. During my journey, I saw many kingdoms, each with its own peculiarities. Some had too many rulers, while others were plagued by fearsome beasts.

I travelled where I wanted to and did as I pleased. However, one gloomy day, my adventurous wandering was suddenly disrupted when I found myself taken into captivity. I had been minding my own business, prowling a particularly nasty kingdom when suddenly someone snatched me. I yowled and hissed and screamed but they did not care. They shoved me into someplace dark and later confined me in a cage, putting me on display for all to see, like I was some ordinary curiosity.

Can you imagine? Me! Royalty! Treated like an average commoner.

It was a very difficult time for me and no matter how hard I tried, I simply could not escape their clutches. However, a glimmer of hope emerged one day when a young human couple were passing by, and they stopped. It seemed like they recognized my noble lineage and regal heritage. I was worried, after so much time in a cage and being on display, I didn't know what to expect. However, they came into the place where I was kept under the clever disguise of being average shoppers. One of them however came to me and whispered, "Don't worry, we will get you out of here, just hold on!"

Perhaps there was hope after all.

I waited for them to come back and did not mind them taking their time. After all, I knew they had to be quite sneaky in liberating me from my captors. They strolled into the shelter and as one of them distracted my captors at the counter, the other unlocked my cage. She then placed me in an undignified cage, hoping not to draw any unusual attention to themselves or to me. She then covered my cage with some cloth as they carried me away. I stayed cautious, my instincts alert, so as to not be caught off guard.

Undoubtedly, their plan was to set me free and usher me into a brand-new kingdom of my own, where I could reign in all my royal splendor, and that is exactly what they did.

Regrettably, this new kingdom turned out to be the tiniest one I had ever set foot in, with no access to the outside world. It felt like some sort of indoor prison, confining me to its limited space.

Just when I thought things couldn't get any worse, a door swung open, and in came two rather smelly dogs, running toward me with great excitement. They wasted no time, initiating their usual routine of sniffing around and attempting to coax me into running from them. After a while, they gave up and left me alone and realized that I would not give in. Of course, by then, I had learned the tricks of dealing with dogs. I knew they were just waiting for that perfect moment to startle me enough to send me running. You see, for dogs, it's all about the chase—quite boring if you ask me!

But the real shocker came when yet another door creaked open, and the most terrifying creature I had ever encountered during all my travels lumbered toward me. It was utterly horrifying! This beast appeared to have no visible fur; instead, it had just a bulky white cloth wrapped around its hind legs, which gave it an odd waddling appearance, like a duck from behind.

This tireless creature seemed to have boundless energy as it pursued me all over my newfound, terribly small kingdom, without pause. In such confinement, I had no choice but to resort to jumping onto tables and counters, seeking higher ground where I could sternly gaze down at this screeching menace while maintaining a semblance of dignity.

Shaking with excitement, screaming as it chased me around and around the indoor maze of furniture,

"Git kitty, Git kitty!" it screamed over and over until eventually one of my new, rather slow-witted, attendants, not exactly the most attentive, came and scooped me up and set me safely on a shelf in a closet, where I was out of sight.

Unfortunately, the closet turned into my makeshift throne. During this period, I learned to become a creature of the night. From my lofty closet perch, I could safely and easily observe all the corners of my realm. It was here that I made a peculiar discovery: the two-legged creature, which I had come to fear, was nowhere to be seen between sunset and sunrise. And as for the two smelly dogs, they were in a deep sleep when my attendants retired for the night.

In the darkness of the night, I found a newfound freedom. I could move about without a care, enjoy my meals in peace, and even use the bathroom without any fear of being chased away at the most critical moments. The night became my canvas, and I roamed about freely, discovering different little things that entertained me during these few peaceful, quiet hours that I enjoyed without those horrible creatures.

During one of my nightly prowls around my kingdom, I stumbled upon something surprising and reassuring. It was the two-legged monster, now locked behind bars within some sort of wooden cage. This confirmed my suspicion that this creature was indeed a monster, after all. If it wasn't, why else would my attendants feel the need to confine him in this prison? Either way, I was happy. I no longer had to deal with this terrible creature.

One fine day, a tall two-legged woman from a distant land arrived at my small kingdom and happened to spot me in my closet hideaway. I could see the sorrow in her eyes as she gazed upon me, confined in such a small space. She was obviously deeply moved by my beauty and regal lineage, which was something that impressed most people. She couldn't resist taking a picture of me to remember the moment.

This kindhearted woman decided to stay for a while, visiting with my attendants and that mysterious two-legged monster—perhaps they were all connected somehow, distant relatives I suppose. As night fell upon the land, and the feasting and merriment faded away and came to an end, the gentle lady took me into her careful hands and placed me inside a mesh tent. Without uttering a word, she whisked me away on a journey that lasted through the night.

After a long ride, she delivered me into the loving embrace of my current attendant. Over the course of two weeks, we got to know each other, forming a deep bond. Finally, the time came for me to behold the splendor of my new kingdom. Here, there were no smelly dogs or menacing two-legged beasts. I could roam freely, both day and night, without anyone disrupting my peace! I knew in my heart that I had found my true home at last.

CHAPTER 3: A SPECIAL PLACE

My other attendant is a gentle giant, a towering figure who fell in love with me and my female attendant just by looking at a picture of the two of us together. In that picture, I sat comfortably on her lap while she gazed at me with absolute adoration—it was clear who held her heart: it was me, naturally. The photo perfectly captured the essence of our special relationship, and he wished to be a part of my home and kingdom.

Had it been anyone else, I would have had my suspicions. Don't get me wrong; even him I had my doubts about initially. However, what I found to be truly astonishing is that he seems to adore my female attendant as much, if not more, as she seems to adore me. I never thought a higher level of love was possible, but this man has shown me otherwise. The remarkable part for me is that he generously extends his loving affection not only to her but also to me. This is why he was welcomed with open arms and granted complete access to my kingdom.

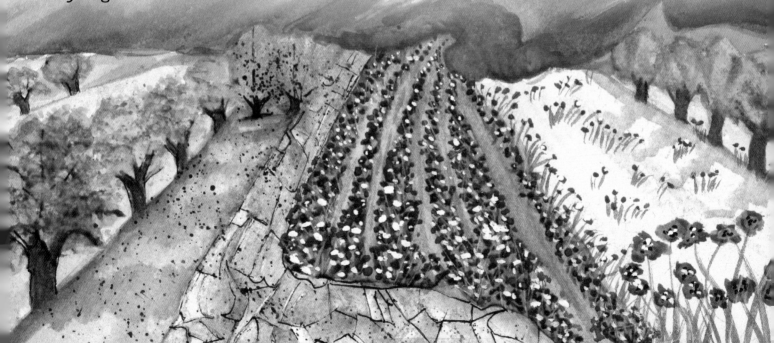

Regarding the arrival of young Capo, I must admit that I'm grateful for the reminder that he has brought me, that despite having lived through most of my nine lives, I still possess a fair amount of spunk. This newfound energy is something I appreciate, although I'm not very enthusiastic about his constant invitations to engage in what he calls "playing."

"Playing," I sneer every time he invites me to tumble.

He's a solid bundle of muscle, with long, robust legs that allow him to roll me around as effortlessly as he does the squirrels. Our wrestling matches often turn into something resembling sparring matches, where I'm forced to use my claws and make vocal protests—a waste of energy, which can certainly take away from the enjoyment of it all.

Often I find myself shouting at him, "Why don't you pick on someone your own size?" when he playfully pounces on me for "fun."

Occasionally I blurt out, "We're not evenly matched! Why don't you go back to where you came from?"

Afterward, I sometimes regret my words because they seem rather harsh, but the regret never lasts too long, for he's not one to back down so easily. He always has a response or a swift retort, reminding me, "Remember, I'm here to serve you, and I'm just a kitten who needs someone or something to play with."

Sadly, it seems that Mr. Capo hasn't quite understood the special nature of this kingdom. You see, Hawks' Haven was meticulously designed from the very beginning as a sanctuary, a place of solace and refuge for a wide range of birds. Every effort

has been made to carefully plant and nurture vegetation that attract a diverse range of birds, and indeed, all forms of life are welcomed here with open arms. In this haven, not only are offerings of animals unnecessary, but they are also viewed as acts of violence and a sign of disrespect toward life itself.

I found myself speaking out loud, rehearsing what I might say to Mr. Capo to get him to understand the importance of this place, "I've had the privilege of reigning as the queen over this remarkable kingdom," I would say, "but it's not just because of my status. It's because I've managed to overcome the instinct to kill for sport. Instead, I find joy in my daily chittering conversations with the winged ones."

I continued to speak softly to myself as I sat there, resting in the cool shade of the weeping cherry tree. "As the queen of this land, it is my responsibility to find a solution to this particular problem. But what can I do? What steps should I take?"

These thoughts kept swirling inside my mind even as I found myself drifting into the embrace of a delightful nap, my mind continuing the rehearsal. "Even though Capo believes he is here to serve me, his actions are unwittingly causing great sorrow and a sense of emptiness in the kingdom. The loss of our feathered friends and the absence of our native songbirds have created a void. It's as if only the most aggressive birds remain here now. The native birds are no longer safe here and are too frightened to return to this place, which has served as a sanctuary for many generations."

Finally, I drifted off into peaceful dreams, free from any worries or concerns, for quite a long while. It was only when Capo stealthily made his way through the Irises and pounced on me that I was stirred from my sleep.

With a calm demeanor, I acted as if I had been expecting his arrival. "Mr. Capo," I announced, gently maneuvering out from beneath his tough body and meticulously straightening my elegant fur, "there's something I need to discuss with you."

In his characteristically sassy manner of addressing me, Capo responded, "Alright, Dulce. What's been weighing on your royal mind?"

"You see, Mr. Capo," I began, "I think that you can rule your own kingdom someday."

I let this thought hang in the air, letting it settle gently upon his young mind.

The idea of seeing himself as a ruler seemed to intrigue Capo. His eyes lit up with curiosity as he said, "Me? A ruler of lands? Wow! Tell me more. I've never really thought about it before."

With a touch of intrigue coloring my words, I began to explain to Capo that there were kingdoms out there where he could truly have a great time. I didn't bother telling him that these were kingdoms where only the most aggressive birds like jays, mockingbirds, and starlings lived. These were places where he would find daily challenges, where he'd have to put in some real effort to secure his prey, instead of easily snatching hummingbirds and finches from the sky as if they were candies on a shelf.

Eagerly, he inquired, "What do I need to do to find myself one of these kingdoms?" His youthful impatience was plain to see.

"You'll need to go on a quest of your own," I responded, my voice trailing off as I began thinking of my own adventures from many lives ago.

Lost in thought, I could see that he too was beginning to imagine his own dreams of future kingdoms.

The following day, we gathered for a heartfelt farewell celebration in honor of Capo. It was a chance for everyone to say goodbye to him and give him their warm wishes for his upcoming adventure. With a touch of ceremonial flair, his vibrant collar was carefully removed. Festive ribbons fluttered in the air as tears welled up in many eyes. A sense of relief and gratitude washed over me as I reflected on the renewed sense of liveliness and zest for life that his presence had brought me.

The news of Capo's departure spread fast and once again, Hawks' Haven was filled with the melodious songs of the juncos, towhees, cedar waxwings, finches, and hummingbirds. Even the charming western bluebirds made their return, gracing us with their presence. It was a delightful treat! In between my daily naps in the warm sun beneath my favorite bushes and trees, I chittered and chatted with my feathered friends, extending a warm welcome to each one of them.

The earlier heaviness that had settled over the kingdom was replaced by the lively tunes of birdsong and the graceful aerial acrobatics that painted the sky above the blooming flowers and lush fields. As I stretched and yawned, I said to myself with a sense of purpose, "Now, it is once again my role to bring smiles to the faces of those around me with my own playful and surprising tricks."

CHAPTER 4: NEWS FROM ABROAD

News from the outlying kingdoms arrived swiftly, carried by winged messengers who brought word of Capo's whereabouts and the woes he now faced. One day, a falcon sentry came, perching on a nearby post. From this vantage point, he could survey the entire land and deliver a comprehensive report.

With a raspy voice, the falcon began to share the details. "Mr. Capo may not be the brightest tool in the shed, but he certainly possesses a great deal of ambition," he remarked.

Eager to learn more, I respectfully implored, "Please, share all that you know."

"Being young, inexperienced, and brimming with playfulness, Mr. Capo stumbled into a treasure trove of feathered playmates. His quest led him into the heart of Falcons' Crest territory."

The falcon, ever watchful, took a moment to look around the area, maintaining his vigilance. Falcons are truly magnificent creatures, known as the swiftest animals on Earth, both in the sky and on land. I encouraged him to continue, after which he resumed his narrative.

"We received immediate notification when Mr. Capo began "playing" with the finches, fragile creatures with bodies that offer them little protection against his mighty claws and teeth," the falcon continued. "Regrettably, his youthful enthusiasm and instinct nearly brought an end to the life of one of these delicate birds. However, our eagle-eyed queen, pardon the pun, spotted his actions, and swooped upon his misguided playfulness with ferocious restraint. She gently carried the injured bird to our infirmary, then went to meet with the wise elders to deliberate on Mr. Capo's fate."

Pausing for a moment, the falcon seemed on the brink of a nap, but suddenly, he raised his head high, reached under his wing, and retrieved a scroll. With an air of importance, he unfurled it and began to read.

"It has been decided," the falcon conveyed solemnly, "that during the day, Mr. Capo will be held in captivity to ensure the safety of the smaller songbirds as they go about their business. However, at nightfall, he will be granted his freedom, as the darkness provides a safeguard against him causing harm to the few larger nocturnal birds. If, for any reason, this arrangement proves unsuccessful, then he will be held in captivity for the entirety of his days and nights." The falcon meticulously rolled his scroll and tucked it away, his voice falling silent once more.

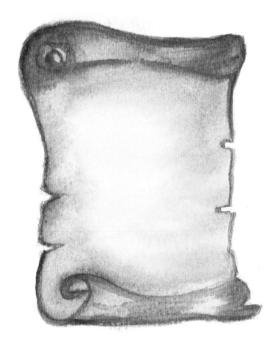

I nodded in understanding and appreciation. "Indeed, it may seem like a rather harsh measure for a young cat, but I do hope that Mr. Capo will come to recognize the mercy that has been extended to him. I'm deeply thankful and grateful for your thorough report and for your queen's compassionate efforts in protecting lives in the most humane way possible. Here at Hawks' Haven, we share a similar sentiment. We wholeheartedly welcome our feathered friends and want to create an environment where they feel secure and can thrive while sharing the abundance of the land. I had encouraged Mr. Capo to go on a quest of his own, so that he may find a more suitable kingdom and it appears that he still has some growing up to do before he's truly ready."

The falcon sentry listened intently and then, with a graceful bow, lowered his majestic wings, and with one mighty downbeat, he ascended ten feet above me. A couple more powerful strokes of his wings, and he seemed to vanish into the distance, leaving behind a display of grace unlike any I had ever witnessed before.

CHAPTER 5: AFTER THE RAINS

*A*fter several weeks had passed, and the rain had finally stopped, I decided it was time to pay a visit to Capo and check on how he was managing in his stay at Falcons' Crest. Setting out on a cool evening after a satisfying meal, I began my journey toward that distant kingdom. With his sleek black coat, Capo wouldn't be easy to spot in the darkness of night, but I knew he was easily distracted by opportunities to play, which might help me locate him more swiftly.

As I approached Falcons' Crest, it wasn't long before I heard the telltale rustling of bunchgrass, undoubtedly a result of Capo's playful pursuit of some small creature. "Hey, Dulcinea! What brings you out here in the dead of night?" He called to me in his typically smooth and easygoing manner. He lay still for a moment, licking his fur smooth after his romp through the grass left it tussled.

Speaking softly from the shadows, I replied, "Well, my dear Mr. Capo, I've come to see how you're managing during your time in captivity."

His white whiskers seemed to glow in the gentle light of the half-moon. It was a relief to see that captivity had not lessened his ability for enjoyment and amusement.

"You see, Mr. Capo," I began, "falcons have long memories and a strong sense of loyalty to their own kind. To save yourself from the hot water you've landed in, you'll need to be on your best behavior."

He shot me a glare, but I pressed on.

"We are, without a doubt, creatures guided by instincts. There's no denying that fact. However, it's important to realize that we have more than the few basic instincts you choose to rely on right now. In my later lives, I've come to realize the importance of one particular instinct—one that has changed my life: love. I only wish I had discovered it earlier, but I'm very grateful to have found it at all. Love has led me to the most extraordinary kingdom, a possibility I couldn't have imagined before I properly accepted and understood the concept of love."

I paused for a moment, allowing my words to resonate within Capo. His curious eyes hinted that he had something to add, but he waited.

"Many of these two-legged beings who tend to our needs are also in the process of nurturing their own instincts for love," I continued. "Admittedly, they may not do a great job in the beginning, but they are willing to go to great lengths to provide us with care and security, all the while practicing love with us. You see, with these human attendants, we can all be winners."

Capo thought for a moment, then he said "You know, I caught a glimpse of that with your attendants and it felt good, but it was kind of strange and boring, lying around on laps purring, even though the caressing eventually feels quite wonderful. The problem with your attendants is that they have such a hard time sitting still and just when I was in dream land, they'd get some idea about something that had to be done, and then I was nearly flying off their laps, landing wide awake on the ground." He said with some frustration.

"Well, it's true. I've come to appreciate those moments with our human attendants. And I've picked up a few tricks to get them to sit down, which I'd be more than willing to share with you. Of course, it does require a willingness to nurture that instinct to love, a trait that exists in all creatures to some degree. It demands a commitment to nurture the growth of love while gradually letting go of other instincts."

He appeared to be pondering my words, his thoughts drifting into reflection. However, in a sudden twist, a mischievous glint danced in his wide, yellow eyes, and without warning, he launched himself into the air, hurtling toward me with all his feline grace. He pounced on me with full force, and we tumbled together for a few feet until I decided to put an end to our roughhousing with a sharp, decisive growl and hiss. I brushed off my fur and gracefully retreated into the night.

As I walked away, disappearing into the shadows, Capo called out to me, his voice filled with sincerity. "Thank you for coming, Dulce! I truly appreciate it, and I'll give your words some serious thought."

CHAPTER 6: NEW POSSIBILITIES

A few months later, two close friends of my attendants paid us a visit. They approached me with a deep look of respect in their eyes and inquired about the possibility of Capo making a visit to their lands, located on the opposite side of the river. I took a deep breath and explained to them the current circumstances and told them that Capo was undergoing a period of captivity at Falcon's Crest.

To my surprise, the news didn't seem to disturb them, and they didn't mind waiting until nightfall, when I could go to speak with Capo about their wonderful offer. It became quite apparent that these two individuals were driven by love and held a profound admiration for feline nobility.

They spent a delightful afternoon with my faithful and beloved attendants, sharing in the joys of food, music, and conversation. As night gradually fell upon the land and the full moon began its ascent in the eastern sky, I took the opportunity to slip away quietly in search of Capo. Upon entering the territory of Falcons' Crest, I scanned the surroundings

and listened intently for the calls of the night-flying owls, seeking their assistance in locating Capo. In the bright moonlight, I was easily visible to the vigilant owls.

"Who . . . goes there?" they called out inquisitively.

"It's Dulcinea, from Hawks' Haven, on a quest to find Mr. Capo," I responded, my voice carrying through the night.

"Ah, good to see you again!" one of the owls chimed in. "He's over there, trying his luck at catching a mouse before we do. He's quite speedy, that's for sure. Sometimes, he tries to get into a playful game with them, wearing them out to the point where they can't escape from us. He's proven to be quite helpful."

I sighed softly before delivering the news. "Well, I'm afraid you'll have to manage without him. He's on his way to establish his own kingdom at long last, ensuring that the birds in your territory will have one less predator to look out for." I paused briefly. "I would greatly appreciate it if you could let your queen know so that she doesn't have to spend her time flying, searching for him."

The owls responded with enthusiasm, their voices filled with goodwill. "Of course, Dulcinea, we're more than happy to assist. Farewell and safe travels!" With that, they gracefully took flight into the night, leaving me to continue my journey.

Capo, who had overheard our conversation, suddenly emerged from the nearby bushes, poised and ready to pounce on me. However, my stiff and unyielding posture clearly showed that I was in no mood for play. Wisely, he decided to stand down and wait for me to speak.

"I've come with an offer of freedom and a chance to establish your very own kingdom," I stated firmly. "But you must come with me now, and we must move swiftly."

As we travelled through the night, I continued our conversation, my tone gentle yet determined. "You see, love is the most important instinct of all, while the other instincts serve their purposes when needed. As you learn to love freely, both giving and receiving, those other instincts will naturally fade away, eventually falling by the wayside. When we embrace love, we discover that without it, nothing else truly matters."

Capo, ever inquisitive, quickly chimed in, "Well, you know, these days, my hunting is more about having fun. I just want to enjoy myself and play. Sometimes, I don't even eat what I catch. So, what about having fun and the need to play?"

I contemplated his question for a moment, my thoughts weaving a response.

"When love is your strongest instinct, fun and play are no longer at the expense of other living things. Hunting becomes a job to do only when the rodent population gets out of hand because these darn humans, who roam the earth, live out of balance with nature. They have not developed their own instincts to love, nor to be loved, and, unfortunately, they do much harm to our beautiful planet." I left off speaking because I knew this young mind would need time and experience to really see and feel the truth of my words.

Upon our arrival at Hawks' Haven, we were met with a heartwarming reception in the grand hall, where my attendants and Capo's soon-to-be companions eagerly awaited us. As we entered, they all rose to their feet in a display of respect and welcome.

I made a beeline for the water, my throat parched after our evening journey and the lengthy conversation we'd had along the way. Meanwhile, Capo stood frozen in his tracks,

his wide eyes filled with a mixture of surprise and gratitude as he gazed up at his new family. These kindhearted individuals were rescuing him from his period of captivity, offering him a fresh start in life and the opportunity to learn the true meaning of love.

The woman knelt down slowly, her demeanor radiating love and tenderness as she carefully lifted Mr. Capo into her soft arms, cradling him on her lap. The affectionate way she handled him, and the soothing strokes she left upon him, were enough to bring tears to my eyes. It was a touching reminder of the initial love and affection I had experienced from my attendant many years ago, a sentiment that had shaped my life so heavily.

As Capo settled comfortably into the woman's lap, gazing up at her with his big, wide eyes, a sense of hope washed over me. I hoped that just as my instincts to play with and catch birds had gradually waned and fallen away with time and by practicing love, the same transformation would occur in Capo.

The kindhearted people carefully loaded Capo into their car. As they drove away, Capo and I locked eyes, a silent understanding passing between us until they disappeared around the corner, leaving us out of sight.

In the days that followed, time seemed to pass slowly, filled with a mix of curiosity and anticipation regarding Capo's adjustment to his new world. My attendants provided me with updates they received from across the river, sharing stories that painted a picture of Capo thriving and finding happiness in his new surroundings.

Now, it was my turn to find comfort. The call of rest beckoned, and I eagerly looked forward to resuming my role as the ruler of my kingdom. I would once again be surrounded by the sweet melodies of birds, the bustling presence of insects, the vibrant greenery of the plants, and ample opportunities for sunbathing. I couldn't help but chuckle at the playful comment from my male attendant, who often strolled past me affectionately, teasing me about "overcooking my brains" while basking in the soothing sunlight. Hawks' Haven, once again, was an atmosphere of tranquility and welcomed all who entered its serene embrace.

NOTE FROM THE AUTHOR

In the US, outdoor domestic cats kill approximately 1.3 billion birds every year. This makes predation from domestic cats the number one human-caused threat to birds in North America. This is from a combination of owned and unowned cats.

Studies have found that cats may kill as many as 79% of fledglings. Fledglings are particularly vulnerable to cats because they don't have many places to hide in suburban areas. This results in a dramatic decrease in the bird population!

Indoor cats don't kill any birds.

I recommend keeping your domestic cats indoors. These felines are safer there and have less of a chance to prey on native birds. It's simply a better place to be for everyone. However, feral cats do the most damage, and no one is around to make sure they spend most of their time indoors.

Controlling the feral cat population is extremely important to help local birds. Catch and release programs and private efforts to lower the feral cat population quickly is essential. Once all feral cats in a colony have been fixed, their population can decline quite dramatically.

For instance, a cat colony can dwindle to only a few members after 10 years. Feral cats do not have extremely long lifespans. If they don't reproduce, the colony will disappear in only a few years.